KU-464-213

For Hilary Delamere H.C.

For my nieces and nephews, Hannah, Adam, Sophie, Thomas and James G.S.

First published 2022 by Walker Books Ltd, 87 Vauxhall Walk, London SE11 5HJ

10 9 8 7 6 5 4 3 2 1   Text © 2022 Helen Cooper   Illustrations © 2022 Gill Smith

The right of Helen Cooper and Gill Smith to be identified as author and illustrator respectively of this work
has been asserted by them in accordance with the Copyright, Designs and Patents Act 1988.

This book has been typeset in Bembo Educational   Printed in China   All rights reserved. No part of this book may be reproduced,
transmitted or stored in an information retrieval system in any form or by any means, graphic, electronic or mechanical, including
photocopying, taping and recording, without prior written permission from the publisher.   British Library Cataloguing in Publication Data:
a catalogue record for this book is available from the British Library   ISBN 978-1-4063-9720-8   www.walker.co.uk

Brainse Mheal Ráth Luirc
Charleville Mall Branch
01-2228411

SAVING THE BUTTERFLY

HELEN COOPER   ILLUSTRATED BY GILL SMITH

WALKER BOOKS
AND SUBSIDIARIES

LONDON • BOSTON • SYDNEY • AUCKLAND

There were two of them left in the boat.

A little one and a bigger one.

Brother and sister, lost in the dark sea.

They could have died.

The bigger one thought they wouldn't survive.

But they did.

They were rescued.

The little one never remembered much:

kind hands, carrying them to land;

sleeping; while the bigger one did the speaking.

Somehow she sorted everything out.

Someone helped.

Someone else found them shelter.

A broken house.

The bigger one said they were lucky.

They could have lost even more.

Yet they had nothing.

Or almost nothing.

Nothing left from before,

except each other.

The little one didn't think about that for long.

But the big one did.

She couldn't help it.

Months went on.
The little one made friends,
grew strong,
and laughed.
He hardly ever thought about the time before.

But the bigger one couldn't forget.
She felt she shouldn't forget.
Over her mind a shadow fell,
while a squeezing in her chest
made it sometimes hard to breathe.

She hid away in their broken house,
feeling safer there,
in the real dark,
hiding from the dark
in her mind.
After a while she hardly ever
came out.

Brainse Mheal Ráth Luirc
Charleville Mall Branch
01-2228411

The little one didn't know how to help.
He wanted to bring her the outside,
(the beautiful outside)
so he caught a butterfly,
carried it back to their
broken house…

… She told him to set it free.

The little one cried.

And the butterfly wouldn't leave.

It battered and smashed its pretty wings against the walls.

Panicking!

"Give it space," said the bigger one.

"Give it time."

After a while the butterfly tired,

and settled.

Tiptoeing, the little one almost trapped it.

But the butterfly turned on him:

flicking its wings, making an angry whispering sound

and now its rainbow markings seemed like watching eyes.

Frightened, the little one hurried outside.

"Come away," he begged his sister.

He didn't want to leave her there.

Brainse Mheal Ráth Luirc
Charleville Mall Branch
01-2228411

"I can't," said the bigger one. "Not yet."

Rain pattered.

The bigger one waited.

Shadows and worries clutched her again.

Usually she breathed deep and counted to ten.

That day, instead, she counted the colours

on the butterfly's wing,

one colour for each breath.

The butterfly was quiet.

She opened the door…

"Shoo!" she said. The butterfly fluttered twice

around the room. Then landed on her hand.

It wouldn't move.

She knew what she ought to do.

She wasn't ready to go,

but would she ever be?

Breathing deep,

counting the colours on the butterfly's wing,

she stepped into the rain.

Still that pesky butterfly clung to her hand.

Until, she took a huge breath,

and blew.

Then, the butterfly flew.

Up, into a shaft of sun and the arch of a sudden rainbow.

The butterfly didn't look back.

She wished she didn't have to look back,

but memories and shadows called,

from the dark safety in the broken house.

Just then the little one saw her.

And he called her too.

She didn't know if she could reach him as the rainbow faded.

But that day she did.